Goldy Luck
and the
Three Pandas

Natasha Yim • Illustrated by Grace Zong

Charlesbridge

First paperback edition 2015
Text copyright © 2014 by Natasha Yim
Illustrations copyright © 2014 by Grace Zong
All rights reserved, including the right of reproduction in whole or in part in any form.
Charlesbridge and colophon are registered trademarks of Charlesbridge Publishing, Inc.

At the time of publication, all URLs printed in this book were accurate and active.
Charlesbridge, the author, and the illustrator are not responsible for the content or
accessibility of any website.

Published by Charlesbridge
9 Galen Street
Watertown, MA 02472
(617) 926-0329 • www.charlesbridge.com

Library of Congress Cataloging-in-Publication Data
Yim, Natasha.
    Goldy Luck and the three pandas / Natasha Yim ; illustrated by Grace Zong.
        p. cm.
    Summary: One Chinese New Year, her mother sends Goldy Luck to the pandas
next door with a plate of turnip cakes, but the pandas are out and disaster follows.
Includes a recipe for turnip cakes and an explanation of Chinese New Year.
    ISBN 978-1-58089-652-8 (reinforced for library use)
    ISBN 978-1-58089-653-5 (paperback)
    ISBN 978-1-60734-729-3 (ebook)
    ISBN 978-1-60734-629-6 (ebook pdf)
1. Pandas—Juvenile fiction. 2. Chinese New Year—Juvenile fiction.
3. Neighbors—Juvenile fiction. 4. Sharing—Juvenile fiction.
5. Conduct of life—Juvenile fiction. [1. Chinese New Year—Fiction.
2. Holidays—Fiction. 3. Neighbors—Fiction. 4. Pandas—Fiction.
5. Sharing—Fiction. 6. Conduct of life—Fiction.] I. Zong, Grace, ill.
II. Goldilocks and the three bears. III. Title.

PZ7.Y535Gol 2014
[E]—dc23   2012038702

Printed in the United States of America
(hc) 10 9 8 7
(sc) 10 9 8 7

Illustrations done in acrylic on paper
Display type set in Liam by Laura Worthington
Text type set in Goudy Sans BT by Bitstream Inc.
Color separations by KHL Chroma Graphics, Singapore
Printed by Villanti Printers in Milton, VT
Production supervision by Brian G. Walker
Designed by Diane M. Earley

When Goldy Luck was born, her mother said, "Year of the Golden Dragon—very lucky year. This child will have good luck."

"She has a face as round as a gold coin," said her father. "This child will bring great wealth."

But Goldy had neither great wealth nor good luck. In fact, she could never seem to keep money in her piggy bank, and she had a bad habit of breaking things.

One Chinese New Year, Goldy's mother woke her up and sent her to wish their neighbors *Kung Hei Fat Choi*.

"But Ma Ma, I'm still sleepy, and I'm so hungry."

"It'll only take a minute," her mother said. "Mr. and Mrs. Chan would enjoy a visit from you. Take these turnip cakes to share with Little Chan."

"He never shares stuff with *me*," muttered Goldy.

"It's the New Year," her mother warned. "Wash away old arguments and be nice, or you'll have bad luck."

Not *more* bad luck. Last year, she lost the red envelope her grandmother had given her. *And* her best friend moved away.

DEAR GOLD,
HOW ARE YOU?
I MISS YOU SO MUCH.
PLEASE COME VISIT.
♥ XOXOXO

So Goldy walked next door to the Chans'
apartment. She knocked on the door. No
answer. She knocked again. Still no answer.

Goldy gave the door a little push. It swung
open, and she tumbled in, dropping the plate.
Turnip cakes catapulted all over the floor.

"Oh, no!" Goldy cried. A whole plate of turnip cakes ruined! That was bad luck for sure.

She wandered into the kitchen to find a broom.
On the table were three steaming bowls of congee—
a ceramic bowl, a wooden bowl, and a plastic bowl.
Her tummy grumbled.

Surely nobody would mind if she had one *little* bite of rice porridge. She sampled the congee from the ceramic bowl. "Ugh! Too watery."

She tasted the congee from the wooden bowl. "Yuck! Too thick and clumpy."

Then she slurped some congee from the plastic bowl. "Mmm . . . just right!" Before she knew it, she had eaten it all up.

All that congee made Goldy even sleepier than she already was. Maybe she could just rest a bit and wait for the Chans.

She walked into the living room and saw three chairs.

She plunked down on Mr. Chan's massage chair. Something hard steamrollered up and down her back. "Ouch!" she cried, springing to her feet. "Too rough."

Next she plopped into Mrs. Chan's armchair and disappeared into the fluffy pillows. She felt like stuffing in a pork bun. "Oof," she mumbled. "Too soft."

Then she squeezed herself into Little Chan's rocking chair. "Whee!" she shouted as she rocked back and forth.

But she pushed too hard and the chair somersaulted backward. It hit the floor with a splintering CRASH.

"Oh, no!" Goldy exclaimed. "Seven years' bad luck!"

Or was that a mirror?

In either case, she was still so sleepy. She ambled into the bedroom to find a place to lie down.
"Just for a few minutes," she reasoned.

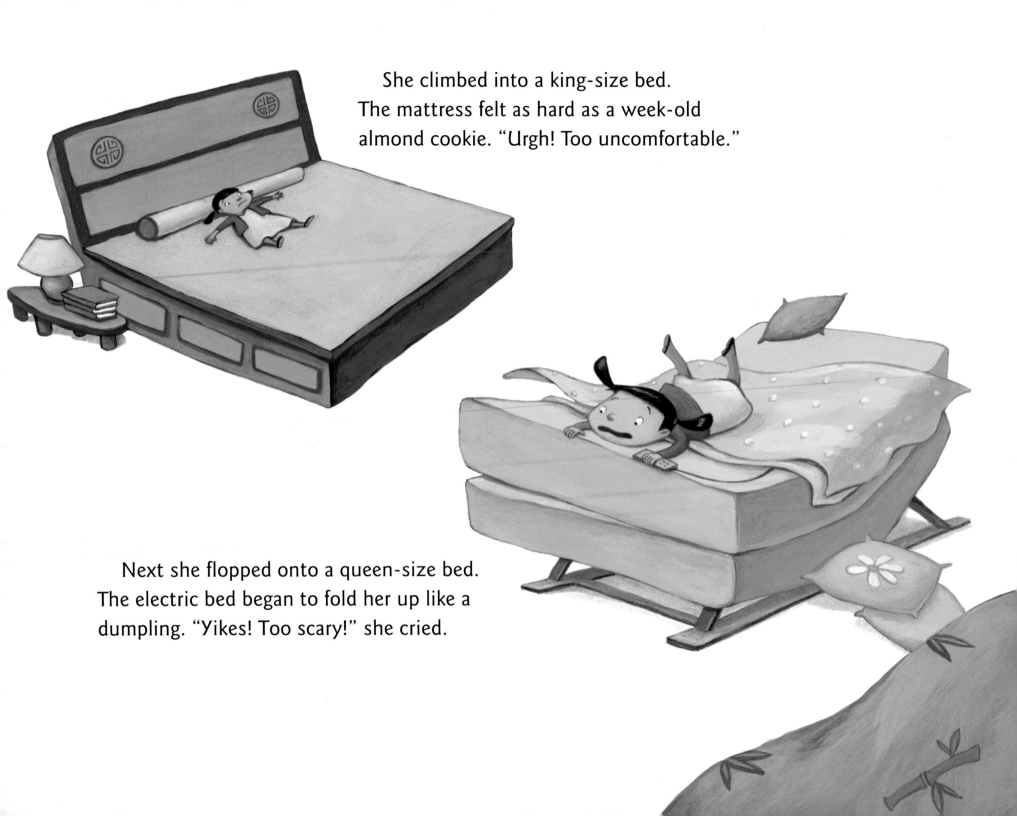

She climbed into a king-size bed.
The mattress felt as hard as a week-old
almond cookie. "Urgh! Too uncomfortable."

Next she flopped onto a queen-size bed.
The electric bed began to fold her up like a
dumpling. "Yikes! Too scary!" she cried.

Then she leaped off and settled down onto
Little Chan's futon. "Aaah, just right," she sighed,
and fell fast asleep.

The Chans finally returned home.
"Who dropped these turnip cakes all over
the floor?" exclaimed Mr. Chan.

"And didn't clean them up?" added Mrs. Chan. "A whole plate of turnip cakes ruined," groaned Little Chan.

They headed into the kitchen.
"Hey, who's been eating my congee?"
demanded Mr. Chan.

"And who's been eating *my* congee?"
cried Mrs. Chan.

Little Chan wailed, "I don't *have* any
congee. Someone's eaten mine all up!"

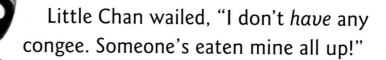

Mr. Chan heard a humming in the living room. He went to investigate. "Someone's turned on my massage chair!" he bellowed.

"And someone's rumpled the cushions on my armchair!" yelled Mrs. Chan.

"I don't even *have* a chair!" shouted Little Chan. "It's been smashed to pieces."

When the three Chans looked in the bedroom, Mr. Chan hollered, "Someone's been sleeping in my bed!"

"And someone's been sleeping in *my* bed!" squealed Mrs. Chan.

"Look," said Little Chan. "It's Goldy Luck, sleeping on my futon!"

Goldy jerked awake. Who could sleep with all that yelling going on?

"Mr. Chan! Mrs. Chan!" she cried. "I didn't mean to fall asleep." In a fluster, she jumped out of bed and dashed home.

Her mother had set out congee for her breakfast. Goldy was just about to take a bite when she thought of Little Chan, who didn't have any more rice porridge in his bowl. "I'm not really that hungry," she said to her mother.

She went to read a book in her rocking chair. As she rocked back and forth, she thought of Little Chan, who didn't have a chair to sit in anymore. "I'm still sleepy. I think I'll go to bed," she said.

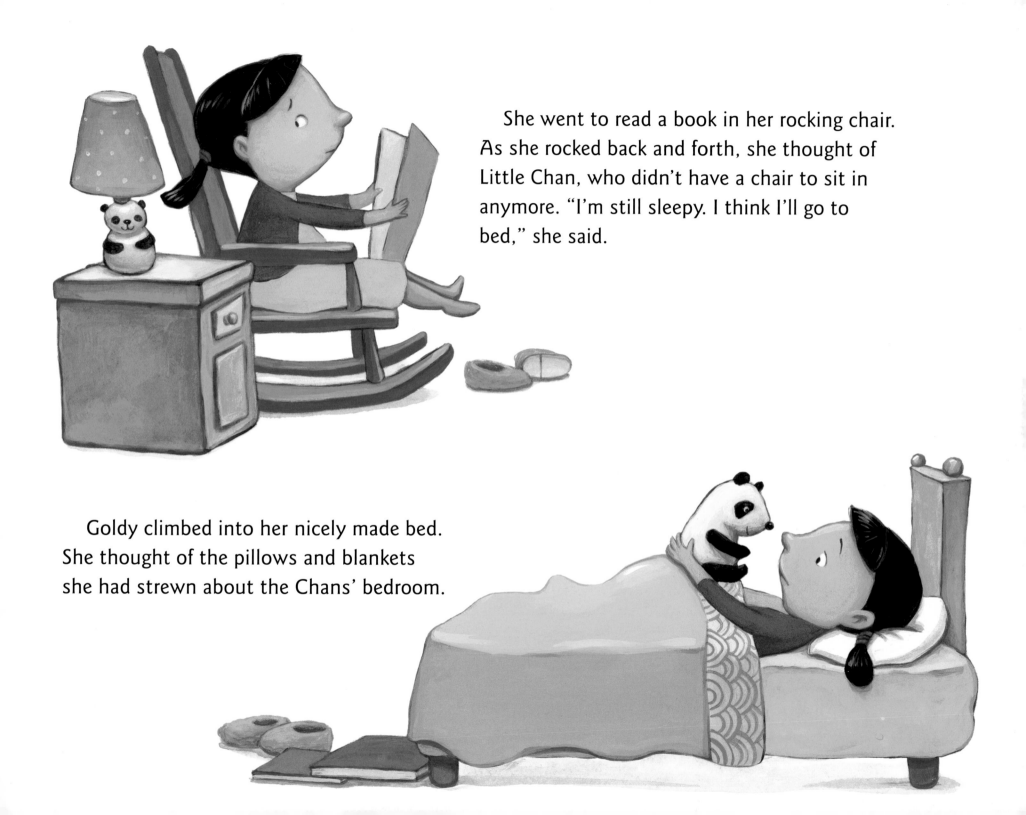

Goldy climbed into her nicely made bed. She thought of the pillows and blankets she had strewn about the Chans' bedroom.

Goldy jumped up and ran back to the kitchen. She grabbed her bowl of congee and rushed back to the Chans' apartment.

"I didn't mean to break Little Chan's rocking chair," she said to Mr. Chan. "I'll help you glue it back together."

"I'll fix the blankets I messed up," she said to Mrs. Chan. "And make the beds."

Goldy handed her bowl of congee to Little
Chan. "I'm sorry I ate all your rice porridge,"
she said, "and dropped all those turnip cakes."

"That's OK, Goldy," said Little Chan shyly.
"We were just about to make some more.
Would you like to help?"

So Goldy and Little Chan chopped, stirred, and steamed lots and lots of turnip cakes. Then they fried them up nice and crunchy for the New Year feast.

Mrs. Chan handed Goldy a red envelope. "*Kung Hei Fat Choi*, Goldy!" she said. "May the New Year bring you great wealth and good luck."

"Thank you," Goldy said. "But I think I've found some good luck already."

She smiled at Little Chan, and the two friends sat
down together to eat a whole plate of turnip cakes.

Author's Note

Good luck, long life, and wealth are important themes in Chinese New Year rituals and preparations. The festival lasts for about fifteen days, beginning on the first day of the lunar calendar. Unlike the Western (or Gregorian) calendar, the lunar calendar is based on the cycles of the moon.

Before New Year's Day it is customary for people to clean their houses, repay their debts, and resolve old arguments in order to start fresh in the new year, as Goldy's mother advises her. However—unless you drop a big plate of turnip cakes on the floor—no sweeping should be done on New Year's Day, lest good luck be swept away.

On New Year's Eve families gather for a holiday meal. They eat foods with special meanings, such as dumplings, fish, noodles, oranges, and—Goldy's favorite—turnip cakes. Dumplings are shaped like old Chinese money and represent prosperity. Fish symbolizes the abundance people hope for in the new year, because the Chinese word for *fish* sounds like the word for *excess*. Long and stringy noodles represent long life. Oranges are round like gold coins and are supposed to bring great wealth. Turnip cakes represent prosperity and rising fortune. Although they can be eaten steamed or fried at any other time of the year, turnip cakes are usually fried during Chinese New Year so that they are brown rather than white—an unlucky color in Chinese culture.

Red, on the other hand, is considered a lucky color in Chinese culture, so many New Year decorations are red. Older and married people give lucky red envelopes containing money to children and unmarried people. The red envelopes are thought to bring good luck to both the giver and the receiver.

Goldy and her family and friends wish each other Happy New Year (*Kung Hei Fat Choi*, pronounced "goong hay faht choy") in Cantonese, a dialect from southern China. In Mandarin, the national language of China, people wish each other *Gong Xi Fa Cai* (pronounced "goong shyee fah tsai") during the Chinese New Year. Either way, it is a wish for friends and family to have good luck and great wealth in the upcoming year.

The Chinese Zodiac

There are twelve animals in the Chinese zodiac: the Rat, Ox, Tiger, Rabbit, Dragon, Snake, Horse, Sheep, Monkey, Rooster, Dog, and Pig. Each animal year comes around every twelve years. There are also five elements in the zodiac: Wood, Fire, Earth, Metal, and Water. Because the Chinese characters for *metal* and *gold* are the same, the Chinese call the Metal Dragon the Golden Dragon. The Year of the Golden Dragon is considered especially lucky because it comes around only once every sixty years.

A Lucky Character

The Chinese character *fook* (or *fu* in Mandarin) means happiness or good luck. During Chinese New Year, it is often hung upside down on the front door because the word for *upside down* sounds the same as the word for *arrive*. When guests come to visit, they say, "Your *fook* (or *fu*) is upside down!"— which sounds exactly like "Your happiness has arrived!"

Turnip Cake

This recipe requires the use of a hot stove and should be made with adult assistance and supervision.

Ingredients

3 cups shredded daikon radish (You can use a food
  processor or hand grater for shredding.)

several tablespoons vegetable or canola oil

2 tablespoons dried shrimp (optional)

1 Chinese sausage (*lap cheong*), finely sliced

2 green onions, finely sliced

2 tablespoons cilantro, finely chopped

2 cups rice flour (DO NOT use glutinous rice flour.
  It will make your dough gooey.)

1 teaspoon salt

½ teaspoon sugar

¼ teaspoon ground white pepper

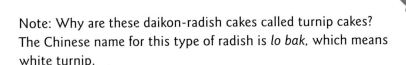

Note: Why are these daikon-radish cakes called turnip cakes?
The Chinese name for this type of radish is *lo bak,* which means
white turnip.

Special thanks to Kirk K. for permission to adapt this recipe
from his blog *mmm-yoso!!!* at **http://mmm-yoso.typepad.com**.

1. Put the shredded daikon radish in a pot. Cover with water (about 3 cups) and bring to a boil. Reduce heat and let simmer for 15 minutes or until tender.

2. While the radish is cooking, heat some oil in a small saucepan. Add the shrimp, Chinese sausage, and green onions. Brown for about 2–3 minutes. Turn off heat and add the cilantro.

3. Drain the radish, but don't throw away the water. Put the radish in a large measuring cup and add the radish water to make 3 cups. Place in a large bowl. Add the rice flour, salt, sugar, and pepper. Mix well. Add the Chinese-sausage mixture and stir. Pour into a square or rectangular baking dish. An 8" x 12" dish works well, but other sizes are fine, as long as the batter is about ½ inch to 1 inch deep.

4. Put 3 cups of water in a large wok or deep roasting pan. Place a steaming rack in the water. (If you don't have a steaming rack, an overturned oven-safe plate or bowl will do.) Set the baking dish on top of the rack, keeping it slightly above the water.

5. Bring the water to a boil. Reduce heat to medium, cover, and steam for 30–35 minutes. Check water level during steaming and add more water as needed to keep pan from drying out. Once the turnip-cake batter has thickened to a Jell-O–like consistency, remove it and let it cool.

6. Cut the turnip cake into squares. Heat some oil in a wok or frying pan and fry the cake squares on both sides until they're brown and crunchy. Enjoy!